Weekly Reader Books Presents

Addie Runs Away

An Early I Can Read Book®

By Joan Robins
Pictures by Sue Truesdell

Harper & Row, Publishers

Addie Runs Away
Text copyright © 1989 by Joan Robins
Illustrations copyright © 1989 by Susan G. Truesdell
All rights reserved. No part of this book may be
used or reproduced in any manner whatsoever without
written permission except in the case of brief quotations
embodied in critical articles and reviews. Printed in
the United States of America. For information address
Harper & Row Junior Books, 10 East 53rd Street,
New York, N.Y. 10022. Published simultaneously in
Canada by Fitzhenry & Whiteside Limited, Toronto.
Typography by Bettina Rossner
1   2   3   4   5   6   7   8   9   10
First Edition

Library of Congress Cataloging-in-Publication Data
Robins, Joan.
  Addie runs away / by Joan Robins ; pictures by Sue Truesdell.
    p.   cm. — (An Early I can read book)
  Summary: Not wishing to be sent away to Camp Putt, Addie is
determined to run away, unless her friend Max can convince her to
change her mind.
  ISBN 0-06-025080-1 : $
  ISBN 0-06-025081-X (lib. bdg.) : $
  [1. Runaways—Fiction.   2. Camps—Fiction.]
I. Truesdell, Sue, ill.   II. Title.   III. Series.
PZ7.R5555Ae 1989   88-24350
[E]—dc19   CIP
                                                          AC

To my mother,
with love

"RUFF, RUFF!" barked Ginger.

Max looked out the window.

5

"Addie," he cried.

"What are you doing

in the doghouse?"

"Shhhhh!" said Addie.

"Come outside."

6

Max ran out to the doghouse.

"What's up?" he asked.

"I am running away," said Addie.

"My parents do not want me."

"How do you know that?"

asked Max.

"I heard them talking last night,"
said Addie.

"They want to send me to Camp Putt—
FOR TWO WEEKS!
I will not know *anyone* there."

9

"Camp Putt!" said Max.

"My Mom and Dad

want to send me there, too."

"Are you going?" asked Addie.

"I can't," said Max.

"Ginger would miss me."

"I don't have *anyone*

to miss me," said Addie,

and she climbed out of the doghouse.

"I have to run away now."

"WAIT!" cried Max.

"*I* will miss you."

"You have Ginger," said Addie.

She took her suitcase.

12

"Good-bye, Ginger. Good-bye, Max,"

she called.

"Miss me forever."

"You will not know anyone

if you run away," yelled Max.

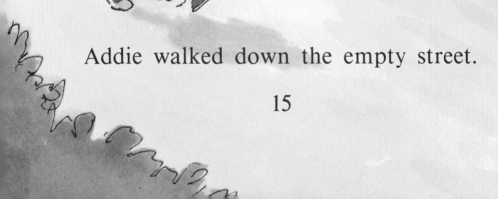

Addie walked down the empty street.

15

"Good-bye, street," she said

at the corner.

"Where are you going
so early in the morning?"
boomed a deep voice
from a big, dark bush.
"EEEK," cried Addie,
and she ran around the corner.

PLOP, PLOP, PLOP.

Someone was running after her!

Addie dropped her suitcase

and hid behind a tree.

19

"It is only me, Addie," said Max.

"You forgot your hat."

"Thank you," said Addie.

"Max, you are still

in your *pajamas*!"

"So what?" said Max.

"Mr. Dill saw you run
around the corner.
You'd better come back,
or he will call your parents."
"RATS!" said Addie.

"Have you ever been to camp, Max?"

"No," said Max.

"But my dad showed me

a picture of Camp Putt.

It has a ball park,

and a big lake,

and . . ."

"Bugs," said Addie.

"There will be

millions of bugs there.

They will crawl all over me.

They will eat me up alive."

"There are bugs here, too,"

said Max.

"Ugh," said Addie.

"Help me carry this suitcase."

"Okay," said Max.

"Let's race back to your house,"
said Addie.

"Last one in

has to go to Camp Putt."

"Whew! This suitcase is heavy,"

puffed Addie.

"Whew! It's hot,"

panted Max.

"Hurry," said Addie,

"before Mr. Dill calls my parents."

27

"RUFF, RUFF!" barked Ginger.

"Home base," yelled Max.

"IT'S A TIE!" yelled Addie.

"We *both* came in last.

Now we *both* have to go

to Camp Putt."

"Ugh!" said Max.

"Ugh-a-bug!" said Addie.

"Ugh-a-bug-a-rug!" said Max.

"Ugh-a-bug-a-rug-a-tug!" said Addie.

"RUFF, RUFF, RUFF!"
barked Ginger.

"Poor Ginger," said Addie.

"She will miss us."

"We'll be back in two weeks,
Ginger," said Max.

"I will bring you a present."

"RUFF!" barked Ginger.

"Giddy-up, pony, giddy-up.

Max and I are going to Putt.

WHOOPEE!" sang Addie.

"RUFF, RUFF!" barked Ginger.